Los Gatos Black on Halloween

Marisa Montes

illustrated by **Yuyi Morales**

HENRY HOLT AND COMPANY ◇ NEW YORK

Los gatos black with eyes of green,
Cats slink and creep on Halloween.
With *ojos* keen that squint and gleam—
They yowl, they hiss . . . they sometimes scream.

Las calabazas, fat and round,
Carved pumpkins guard a hallowed ground.
Their eerie faces burning bright
Form spooky beacons in the night.

Las brujas guide their broomsticks high,

The witches on *escobas* fly.

Above the earth, before the moon,

They swoop and swish and swoosh, and soon . . .

. . . Los esqueletos rattle bones.
The skeletons with creaks and groans
Delight the night, in moonbeams dance—
An awkward bow, a clattering prance.

Next los fantasmas drag their chains;
The ghosts, the phantoms, shriek their pains.
Now come the ghouls. Then zombies march
Beneath the trees where branches arch.

October's *luna*, full and bright,
The fall moon lights a vampire's bite.
La momia walks, the mummy stalks,
And faraway a lone loon mocks.

At medianoche midnight strikes—
The witching hour the werewolf likes.
The bloodhounds bay, *los perros* howl.
Beware! The wolfman's on the prowl.

The gravesites shiver, headstones shake.
Las tumbas open, tombs awake.
The corpses with their cold, dead eyes,
Los muertos from their coffins rise.

And in a slow and strange parade,
The creatures of the night invade
A haunted *casa*, long asleep—
The mansion's secrets buried deep.

Yes, by the magic of this night,
This noche filled with chills and fright,
The monsters crowd the Haunted Hall—
Los monstruos throw a monstrous ball.

On harpsicords once tucked away,
Some unseen *dedos*—fingers—play
Forgotten music, tinkling, clear . . .
La música the dead can hear.

Las brujas boogie, muertos bop,
Los esqueletos do the hop.
The ghosts in their transparent waltz
Glide through the wolfman's somersaults.

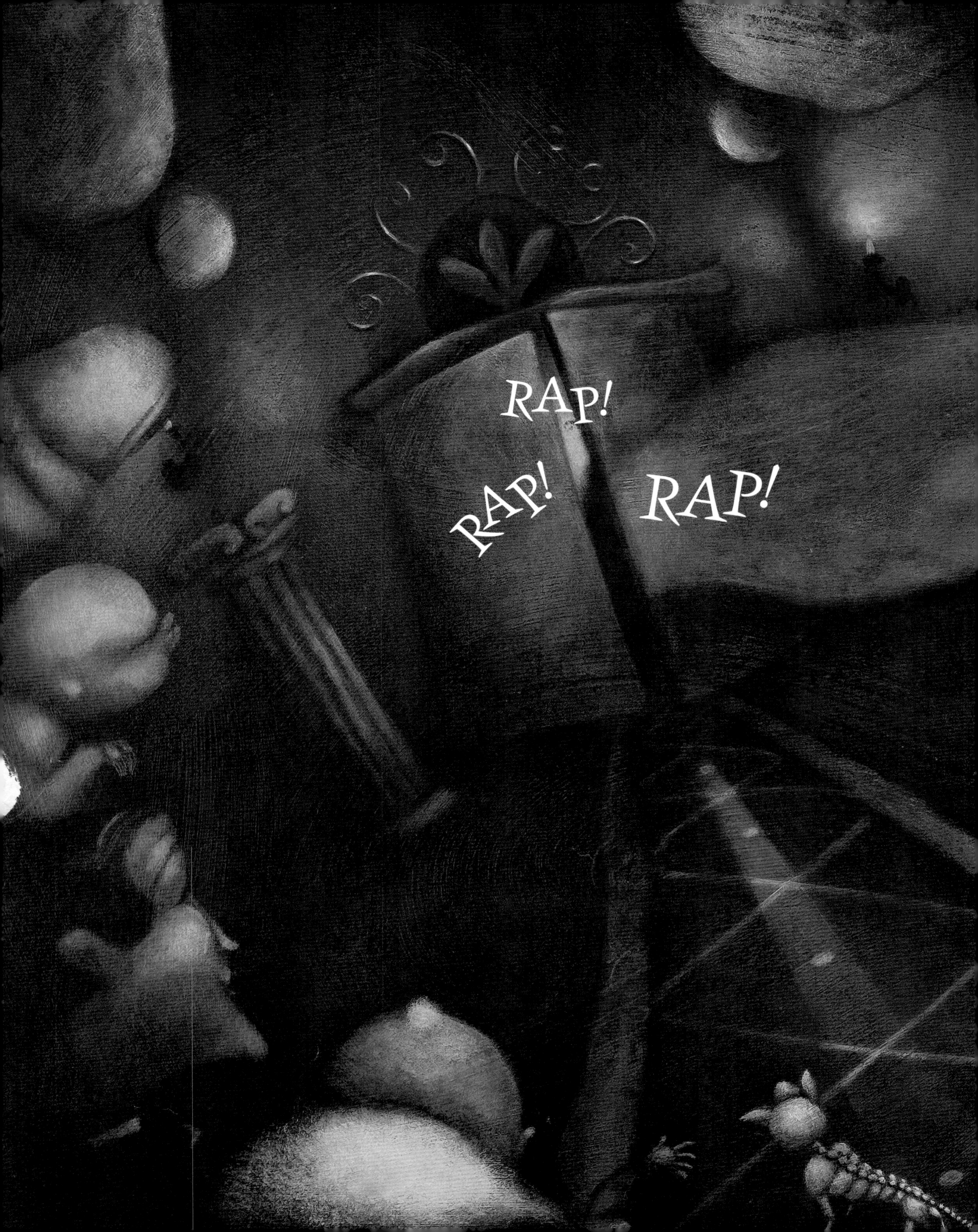
RAP!
RAP!
RAP!

Then from the door come tres loud raps!
What could it be? Is it perhaps . . . ?
The music stops. Each creature gasps.
And suddenly the door unclasps!

La puerta creaks . . . it opens wide.
The things are coming. Run and hide!
They hold up bags, yell "TRICK OR TREAT!"
Los monstruos beat a quick retreat.

The thing that monsters most abhor
Are human *niños* at the door!
Of all the horrors they have seen,
The WORST are kids on Halloween!

GLOSSARY

bruja / las brujas (BROO-hah / lahs BROO-hahs). Witch; the witches.

calabaza / las calabazas (kah-lah-VAH-sah / lahs kah-lah-VAH-sahs). Pumpkin; the pumpkins.

casa (KAH-sah). House.

dedo / dedos (DEH-doh / DEH-dohs). Finger; fingers.

escoba / escobas (es-KOH-vah / es-KOH-vahs). Broom; brooms.

esqueleto / los esqueletos (es-keh-LEH-toh / lohs es-keh-LEH-tohs). Skeleton; the skeletons.

fantasma / los fantasmas (fan-TAHZ-mah / lohs fan-TAHZ-mahs). Phantom; the phantoms.

gato / los gatos (GAH-toh / lohs GAH-tohs). Cat; the cats.

las / los (lahs / lohs). The.

luna (LOO-nah). Moon.

medianoche (meh-deeyah-NOH-cheh). Midnight.

momia / la momia (MOH-meeyah / lah MOH-meeyah). Mummy; the mummy.

monstruo / los monstruos (MOHNS-trwoh / lohs MOHNS-trwohs). Monster; the monsters.

muerto / los muertos (MOOWARE-toh / lohs MOOWARE-tohs). Dead; the dead.

música / la música (MOO-see-kah / lah MOO-see-kah). Music; the music.

niño / niños (NEE-nyoh / NEE-nyohs). Child; children.

noche (NOH-cheh). Night.

ojo / ojos (OH-hoh / OH-hohs). Eye; eyes.

perro / los perros (PEH-rroh / lohs PEH-rrohs). Dog; the dogs.

puerta / la puerta (POOWARE-tah / lah POOWARE-tah). Door; the door.

tres (trehs). Three.

tumba / las tumbas (TOOM-bah / lahs TOOM-bahs). Tomb; the tombs.

*For Tití Carmín
because you have always
believed in me
—M. M.*

*For Tim O'Meara, who taught me
how to love in English:
Yo le adoro con todo mi español
—Y. M.*

Henry Holt and Company, LLC
Publishers since 1866
175 Fifth Avenue
New York, New York 10010
www.henryholtchildrensbooks.com

Henry Holt® is a registered trademark of Henry Holt and Company, LLC.
Distributed in Canada by H. B. Fenn and Company Ltd.

Library of Congress Cataloging-in-Publication Data
Montes, Marisa.
Los gatos black on Halloween / Marisa Montes; illustrated by Yuyi Morales.—1st ed.
p.   cm.
Summary: Easy to read, rhyming text about Halloween night incorporates Spanish words, from las brujas riding
their broomsticks to los monstruos whose monstrous ball is interrupted by a true horror.
ISBN-13: 978-0-8050-7429-1 / ISBN-10: 0-8050-7429-5
[1. Halloween—Fiction. 2. Spanish language—Vocabulary—Fiction. 3. Stories in rhyme.] I. Morales, Yuyi, ill. II. Title.
PZ8.3.M775Gat 2006   [E]—dc22   2005020049

First Edition—2006 / Designed by Laurent Linn
Printed in the United States of America on acid-free paper. ∞

1 3 5 7 9 10 8 6 4 2